THIS BOOK
BELONGS TO:

_____

DATE RECEIVED: _____

D0575682

Deep in the ocean, in the coral reef, among the shipwrecks and seaweed, the ocean creatures live and play. Here is what happened to them one warm and sunny day.

Sindy is a seahorse who loves to show off her backflips. "I am the best in the ocean!" she would often say.

On this particular day,
Connor crab became tired of
her bragging. "You are good
at backflips," he said, "but are
you a fast swimmer?"

"The fastest," said Sindy.
"I am a seahorse, of course."

"If that's true," said Connor,
"then let's have race to prove it!"

"No problem," boasted Sindy, "all you'll see of me is my tail."

Connor rolled his eyes and groaned. "Tomorrow, when the tide is out, through the Coral Canyon. Don't be late!"

"I'll be there!" Sindy said boastfully, even though inside she was really afraid she might lose.

The next day, Sindy, Connor, and their two friends Sid squid and Tory tuna swam up to the starting line outside of Coral Canyon. Gavin green fish waved his fin to start the race. Off they went!

Sindy fell quickly behind. "How embarrassing," Sid remarked. Connor was the first to slow down and let Sindy catch up. After all, that's what friends do.

Just before they went inside the Canyon, Sindy caught up and passed the group. "I told you I was the best!" she called back. Her friends sped up and passed her again.

Soon they were far ahead of Sindy. She decided she'd have to take a short cut, if she was going to win the race.

Sindy was a long way behind
when Tory turned just in time to
see her cutting through the ruins
to get ahead.

"We'd better speed up even
more or Sindy will win this race
by cheating!" said Connor.

Once they got into the canyon, they realized that although Sindy was cheating, she was still behind them.

"Maybe we should let Sindy catch up again," Tory suggested as they neared the finish line. So they all stopped and waited.

When Sindy reached the Coral Canyon, she decided to take a shortcut that would lead her right to the finish line. She was almost through, when she saw the group and hid behind a rock.

"It's sure taking Sindy a long time to catch up to us." Sindy heard Connor say.

When Sindy heard this, she was very ashamed of herself for cheating. She turned and went all the way back to where she first cheated and finished the race honestly.

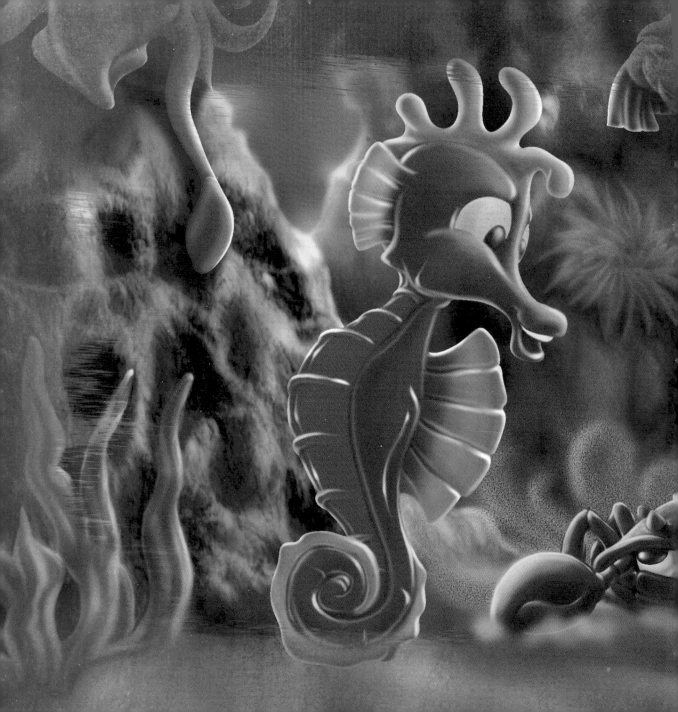